"HELLO READING books are a perfect introduction to reading. Brief sentences full of word repetition and full-color pictures stress visual clues to help a child take the first important steps toward reading. Mastering these storybooks will build children's reading confidence and give them the enthusiasm to stand on their own in the world of words."

—Bee Cullinan
Past President of the International Reading
Association, Professor in New York University's
Early Childhood and Elementary Education Program

"Readers aren't born, they're made. Desire is planted—planted by parents who work at it."

—Jim Trelease
author of *The Read-Aloud Handbook*

"When I was a classroom reading teacher, I recognized the importance of good stories in making children understand that reading is more than just recognizing words. I saw that children who have ready access to storybooks get excited about reading. They also make noticeably greater gains in reading comprehension. The development of the HELLO READING stories grows out of this experience."

—Harriet Ziefert
M.A.T., New York University School of Education
Author, Language Arts Module,
Scholastic Early Childhood Program

VIKING
Published by the Penguin Group
Viking Penguin, a division of Penguin Books USA Inc.,
375 Hudson Street, New York, New York 10014, U.S.A.
Penguin Books Ltd, 27 Wrights Lane, London W8 5TZ, England
Penguin Books Australia Ltd, Ringwood, Victoria, Australia
Penguin Books Canada Ltd, 2801 John Street, Markham, Ontario, Canada L3R 1B4
Penguin Books (N.Z.) Ltd, 182-190 Wairau Road, Auckland 10, New Zealand

Penguin Books Ltd, Registered Offices: Harmondsworth, Middlesex, England

First published in 1991 by Viking Penguin, a division of Penguin Books USA Inc.

1 3 5 7 9 10 8 6 4 2

Text copyright © Martin Silverman, 1991
Illustrations copyright © Amy Aitken, 1991
All rights reserved
Library of Congress catalog card number: 90-50712
ISBN 0-670-83862-4

Printed in Singapore for Harriet Ziefert, Inc.

My Tooth Is Loose!

Martin Silverman
Pictures by Amy Aitken

VIKING

Georgie wasn't playing.
He just sat there.

"What's wrong?" asked Daniel.

"My tooth is loose," Georgie said.
"I don't know what to do!"

"When my tooth was loose,"
Daniel said, "my daddy
took it out with a string."

"I don't want a string!"
said Georgie.

Then Diana came.
"What's wrong?" she asked.

"My tooth is loose," Georgie said.
"I don't know what to do."

"Bite into an apple,"
said Diana,
"and your tooth will come out."

"I don't want to bite an apple,"
    said Georgie.
"It might hurt!"

Then Carol came.
"What's wrong?" she asked.

"My tooth is loose," Georgie said.
"I don't know what to do!"

"Let the dentist pull it out,"
Carol said.

"Oh, no," Georgie said, "I don't want the dentist to pull it!"

"What's wrong?" asked Bobby.

"My tooth is loose," Georgie said.
"I don't know what to do!"

"Twist it!" Bobby said.
"Twist it until it comes out."

"I won't twist it," Georgie said.
"It might bleed!"

"What's wrong?" asked Linda.

"My tooth is loose," Georgie said.
"I don't want a string!
 I don't want an apple!
 I don't want the dentist to pull it!
 And I won't twist it!"

"When my tooth was loose," Linda said, "my grandma gave me fudge. I bit the fudge and swallowed my tooth."

"You swallowed your tooth!" Georgie said.
"I don't want to swallow a tooth.
It might grow inside me!"

Georgie still didn't know
what to do.

"No string!" he cried.
"No apple!"
"No dentist!"
"No twisting!"
"And no fudge!"

"Mama! Mama!" he cried.
"My tooth is loose!"

"Open your mouth," his mother said, "so I can look at your tooth."

"You can look, " said Georgie, "but don't touch!"

"You don't have to do anything," said his mother.
"Your tooth will come out all by itself."

And it did!